Grandma's LOST GIFT

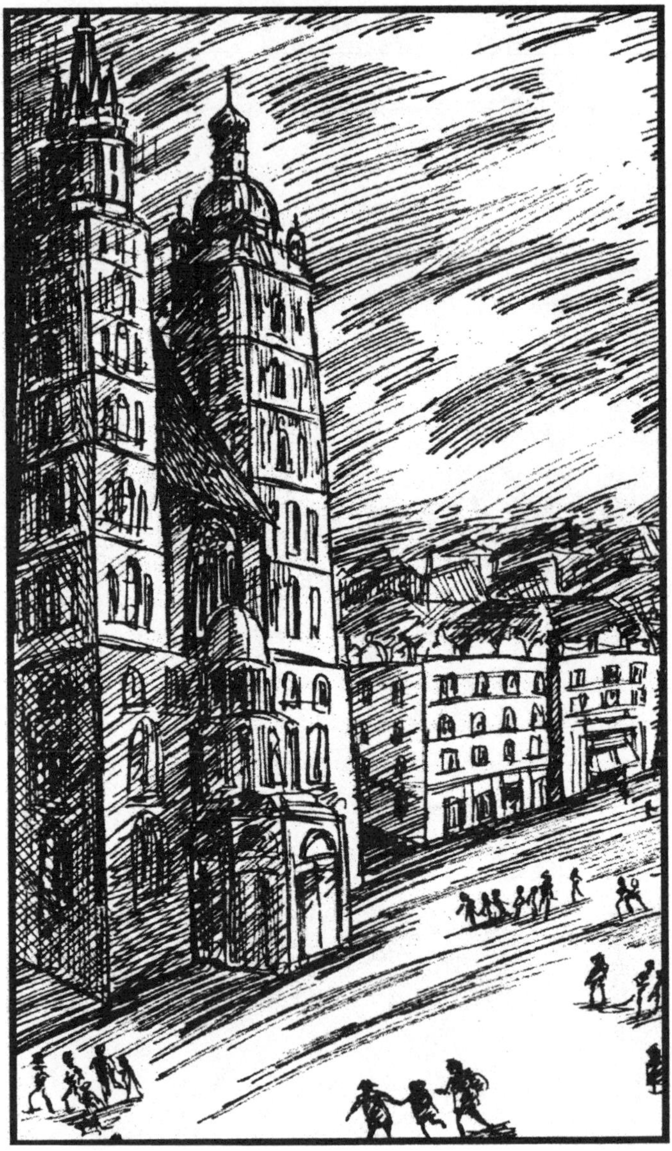

Grandma's LOST GIFT

A CHRISTMAS STORY
by Harvey & Audrey Hirsch

Illustrations by Martha Weston

COBBLESTONE PRESS
A Division of Cobblestone Books, Inc.
Ann Arbor, New York, London

Copyright © 1988, 1992, 1994, 2007
by Harvey and Audrey Hirsch

Previously published as *The Crèche of Krakow*

All rights reserved. No part of this book may be used or reproduced in any manner without prior written permission of the publisher, except in the case of brief quotations embodied in critical articles and reviews.

Manufactured in the United States of America
Illustrations by Martha Weston

COBBLESTONE PRESS
A Division of Cobblestone Books, Inc.
Ann Arbor, New York, London

ISBN: 0-929613-00-7

Printed & Bound By McNaughton & Gunn, Inc.
Saline, Michigan

To our children and grandchildren

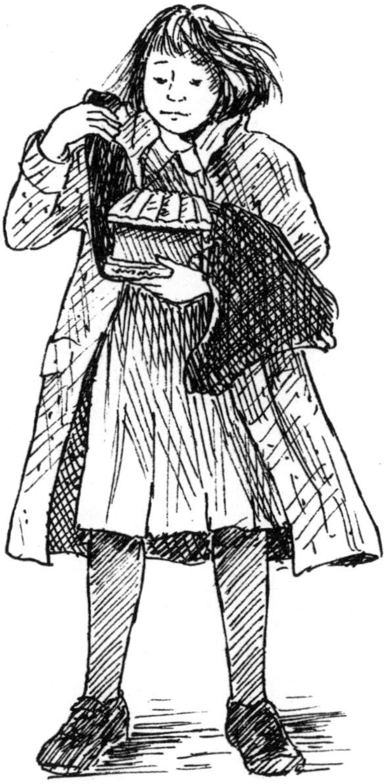

Part I

"On The Eve of War"

Poland, 1939

"Anna!...Anna, wake up!...Wake up!" urged Mrs. Malek, shaking her daughter's arm. "We must leave at once. Hurry! Get dressed. Take your heavy coat. Nothing else. Hurry!"

"But...why?" asked Anna, still not fully awake. "Where...where are we going?"

"They have bombed Warsaw," said Mrs. Malek, her voice trembling with emotion. "Soldiers have crossed the border. They will soon be here in Krakow. We must go to Uncle Juliusz. He will help us. But you must get up and get dressed now! Hurry!" And with that, she turned and left the room.

For a moment, Anna thought she had

been dreaming. She sat up and looked toward the small window at the foot of her bed. The sky was still dark. Silver-white stars twinkled dimly through the lace curtains. She could hear the faint ticking of the little cuckoo clock on her bedroom wall. Had her mother really been there? Had she really told her that soldiers were coming — that Warsaw had been bombed — that they would have to leave…now…in the middle of the night? Or had it all been a dream?

Suddenly, flashes of light and the dull thunder of heavy explosions in the distance filled her room, and Anna knew she was awake. And she was frightened — more frightened than she had ever been before — so frightened she could hardly breathe. All that she had feared — all the terrible dreams — were coming true. For weeks now she had been listening to her classmates and teachers talk about the possibility of war — of soldiers invading Poland. And each night, after she had kissed her mother and father good night, she knew they would sit for hours at the kitchen table, listening anxiously to radio

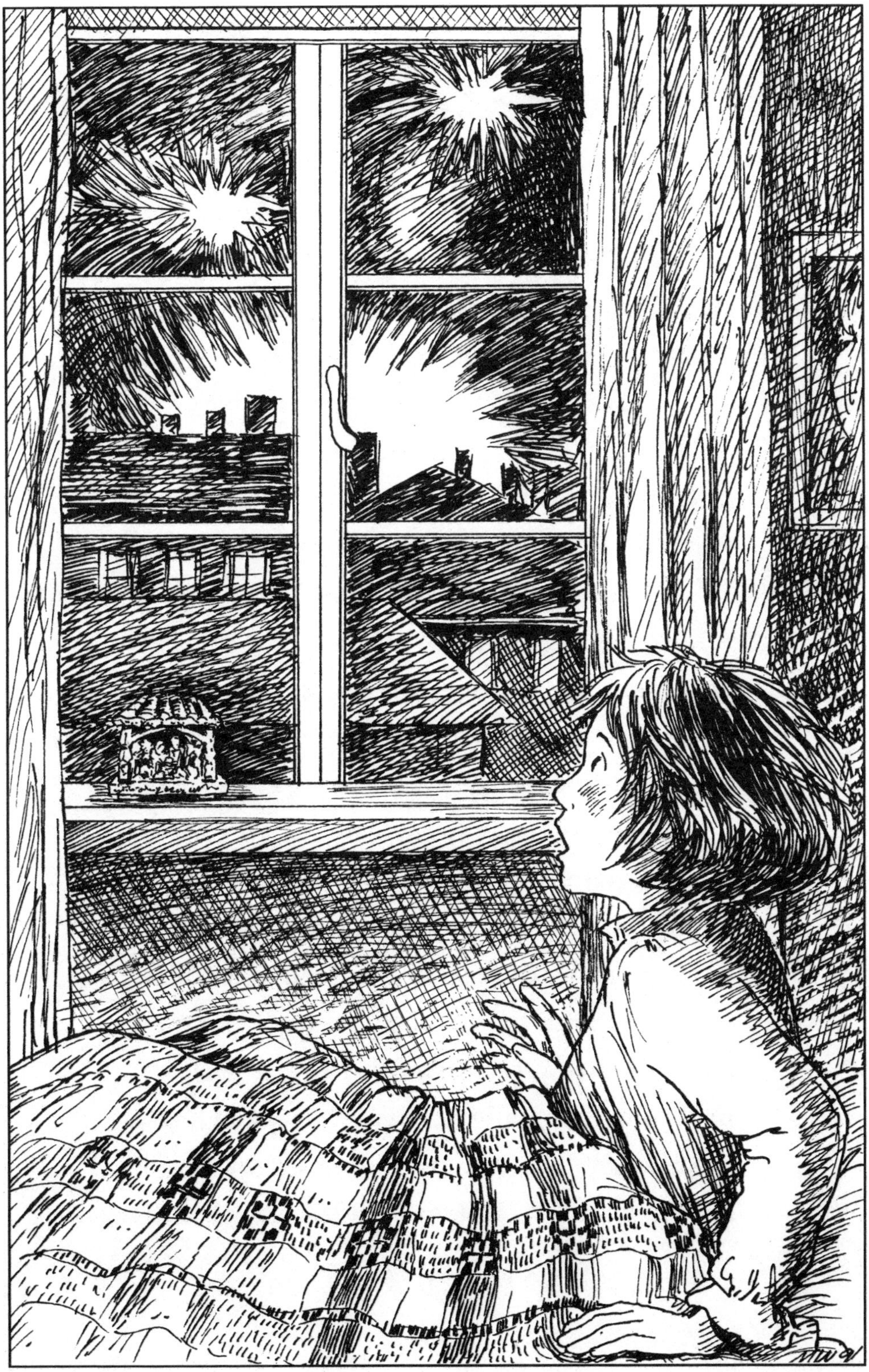

reports telling of the massive buildup of troops and tanks all along Poland's western border.

"Will they really invade?" Anna's mother asked, her voice tense with fear and concern. "What will happen to Anna?"

"Don't be afraid, Helena. It will be all right," her father said. But even as he tried to comfort her mother, Anna knew he was terribly worried, and this made her even more afraid.

Sometimes, as she lay awake listening, Anna could hear the news reporter's voice as it broke through the crackling static of the radio. Although she wasn't always sure of just what the reports meant, she knew that war was a terrible thing. And she was frightened.

Even as these thoughts raced through her mind, there was a sudden loud explosion close by, and Anna could feel the entire room tremble. She threw back the covers, got out of bed, and dressed quickly. She found her heavy coat and put it on. Then, fully dressed, she looked about the room, still unable to believe that she would have to leave everything behind. All of her most special and wonderful possessions. Her soft feather bed, with its red and white quilt. The little blue chest that Grandpa made for her, and on which he had carved and painted flowers and butterflies. Her dolls — all her beautiful dolls — little Lena, with the bright yellow hair, and Tanja, and Marie, and Nadja. Her ivory music box, where she kept the beautiful silver ring with the dark red stone that Grandma Wilna had given to her last year on her tenth birthday. All her clothes — her sweaters, and jackets, and dresses — everything, even her new red dress with the white lace, which her mother had just finished. And her shoes, especially the shiny black patent leather ones with the little heels. She could take nothing — nothing at all.

Then Anna looked at the windowsill, where she kept the crèche that Grandpa Malek had carved for her last Christmas. She ran to the window, and looked closely at the little Nativity scene, with its carved and painted figures of Mary and Joseph. Between them, in a tiny straw-filled manger, lay the Holy Baby. And watching from the back of the crèche were four lambs, a cow, and a donkey.

Anna remembered that wonderful Christmas Eve, when Grandpa Malek gave her the crèche. "This is for you, my dear Anna," he said. And she remembered how his eyes had filled with tears when he handed it to her, and how excited she was as she carefully opened the box in which he had placed it. She remembered clearly how she had parted the soft white paper that surrounded it, and how everyone had watched as she carefully lifted it out of the box. To Anna, it was the most beautiful, the most magically wonderful gift she had ever received. The tiny carved and painted figures and animals seemed so real that Anna could almost imagine herself standing there in the little stable, watching the tiny baby as He slept so peacefully in the soft straw.

"And here," said Grandpa Malek, "is my mark — the letter M — so that someday, when you show this crèche to your children and, perhaps, to your children's children, they will know how very much your Grandpa Malek loved you." And she remembered how, as he spoke, her finger had traced along the ornately carved letter, with its swirls and curves.

"Oh, thank you, Grandpa. It's so beautiful. I will keep it for ever and ever."

Suddenly, Anna felt dizzy and sick to her stomach. "I *can't* leave it," she said aloud. "I *can't*. Poppa will *have* to let me take it. He *must!*" Anna took the crèche from the windowsill and quickly, but carefully, wrapped it in her heavy blue sweater. After tying the sweater arms together to make a tight bundle, she placed it inside her coat.

As she did so, there were several heavy explosions, close enough to shake the building. Several teacups in the kitchen fell to the floor and broke. She heard her mother cry out. Then her father called, "Hurry, Anna. We must go *now*!" Anna ran to the bedroom door. As she stepped into the hallway, she spun around and took one last look at her room. Tears rolled down her cheeks. "Good-bye," she whispered. Then she turned and ran toward the living room, where her parents waited.

A moment later and they were racing down the narrow staircase to the street. The night sky was aglow with red-orange light from several large fires at the edge of the city. Another thunderous explosion shook nearby buildings and loosened the cobblestones over which Anna and her parents hurried. The street was now filling rapidly with people. Many carried suitcases and bundles as

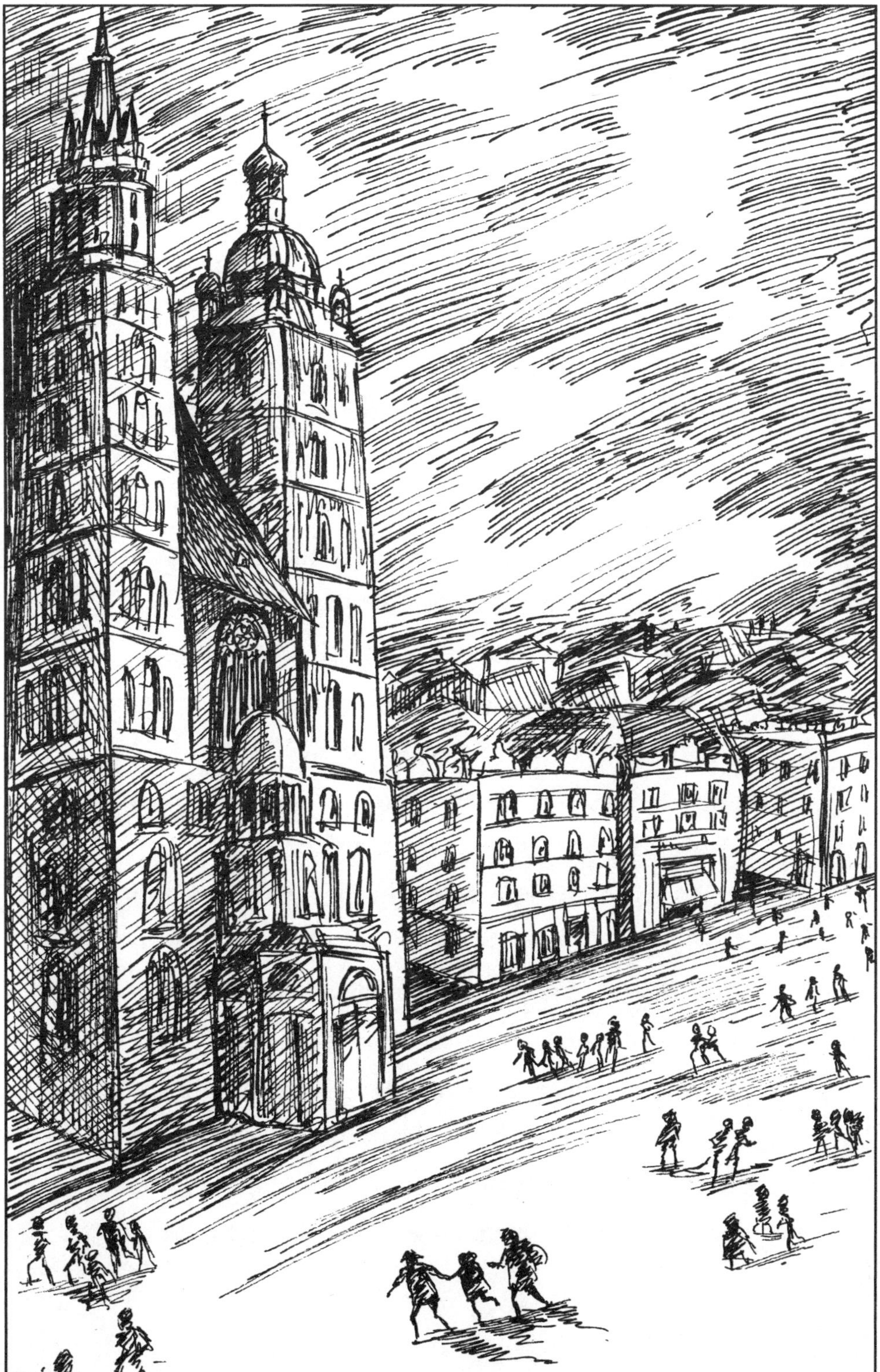

they hurried toward the old city gates. Several heavy trucks rumbled along the street. An ambulance, its warning bell ringing loudly, raced by in the direction of the fires.

"This way," called Anna's father, as he led the family down Florian Street, toward the western gate. At the end of the street, they turned right, and crossed over to the old Rynok Market square. They hurried across the square and past the ancient Church of the Trumpeter, its tall dark towers rising majestically above them.

As Anna hurried by the ancient building, she remembered how she and her family had gathered in front of the old church on Christmas Eve, along with thousands of other Krakow residents, to listen to the four trumpeters, who stood at the top of the high tower and played a beautiful Christmas hymn. The great crowd of people had looked up and listened as each note of the hauntingly beautiful melody echoed across the old city, then floated away on the night air into the Polish countryside.

Then the cold, clear night had seemed to

turn warm as the crowd, which had stood silently, listening to the silvery notes of the trumpets, began to sing. Anna remembered that night and how she had almost cried when the beautiful singing came to an end.

"There," said Anna's father. "There is the gate." Just ahead, Anna could see the gray stone walls of the old Florian gate. Moments later, Anna and her parents hurried through the stone archway. They had left Krakow, and were now on a journey across the Polish countryside, toward Stanislawow and Uncle Juliusz's farm — two hundred miles away.

Part II

"Flight"

Poland, 1939

The hay wagon rocked and bumped as it moved slowly along the narrow dirt road that wound its way toward the southeast and the Rumanian border. Holding tight to her blue sweater, with the little crèche hidden safely inside, Anna snuggled deeper into the hay that filled the old wagon and was soon fast asleep. The late afternoon sky grew more overcast, with dark gray clouds that threatened more of the cold rain that had been falling on and off all day.

Although Anna slept deeply on the gently swaying mound of wet hay, she knew she was hungry. She had not eaten since early that morning. She had had a piece of dry bread and some warm milk from a mother goat Uncle Juliusz found on one of the many abandoned farms they had passed. And perhaps because she was so hungry, Anna began to dream of the bakery near her home in Krakow. It was one of her very favorite places, and she was always eager to be asked to run to the bakery to buy a loaf of bread for supper. Anna loved the delicious aroma of the freshly baked breads and rolls that filled the glass display cases. When she arrived at the shop, she would stand in front of the bay window that faced the street and look at the many different kinds of cookies, cakes, and pastries that filled the large metal trays lined up just inside the shop window. Some were piled high with cinnamon cakes and fat pastries filled with poppy seeds and honey; others held cookies with raisins, nuts, and bits of chocolate. Still other trays were filled with star-shaped cookies, coated with a buttery icing that sparkled with tiny crystals of white sugar.

Anna was also especially eager to be asked to go to the bakery because it was almost

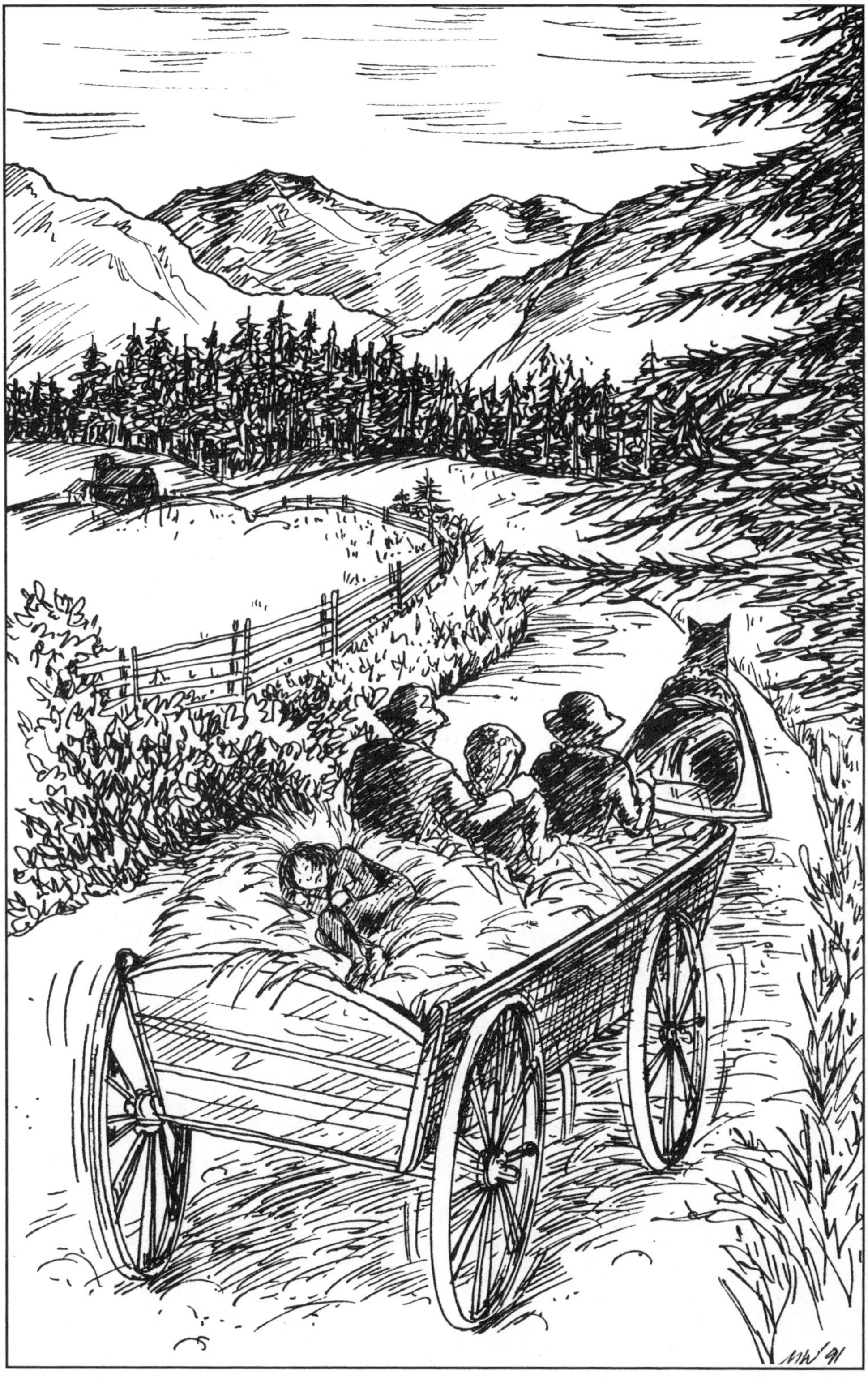

certain that the baker's wife would quietly slip her a sweet pastry or butter cookie to eat on the way home. And Anna made her treat last as long as she possibly could. When she left the shop, she would take only a very small bite, then walk at least one full block before taking another. If the treat was large enough, or if her bites were small enough, she could make the little cookie or pastry last until she arrived at the front door of her apartment building on Florian Street.

In her dream, the baker's wife had given her an especially large pastry filled to overflowing with poppy seeds and honey. It was so large, that Anna could take huge bites without it getting any smaller. And it was so delicious — so very wonderfully delicious. But just as Anna was about to take another big bite, she woke up.

The wagon had come to a stop, and Anna could hear her Uncle Juliusz talking to her father. "This is as close as we can get to the border with the wagon," he said. "There will be soldiers watching the crossing. There is a small farm up ahead. We can stay in the barn until dark, then we can cut across the field to the woods."

"How much farther is it?" asked Anna's father, with concern. "Anna and Helena are so tired. We have been traveling now for almost a week."

"It is only about a mile or so," said Juliusz. "Once we are across the open field and in the woods, we can go slowly."

The wagon moved forward again, rocking and bumping its way along the dirt road until it came to the farm. Here, Uncle Juliusz drove the wagon along a narrow winding path to the front of the barn. The farm, like so many others they had passed, had been abandoned. Everything was still. Anna's father jumped down from the wagon and opened the barn doors wide enough for Uncle Juliusz to drive the wagon forward and into the barn.

"Close the doors," said Uncle Juliusz, as he jumped down from the wagon. "I'll unhitch the horse and look for some water and oats."

Anna's father closed the barn doors, then helped Anna and her mother down from the wagon. "There's some hay in the corner," he said. "You and Anna should try to get some rest, because we will have to walk the rest of the way. Juliusz and I will keep watch."

Anna and her mother sank wearily into the large mound of hay. Anna placed her blue sweater bundle on the hay beside her, and then snuggled close to her mother. "Momma," she said, "I'm so hungry."

"I know, dear. Let me see what I have left." Anna's mother reached into her coat pocket and took out a kerchief in which she had wrapped the last piece of dry bread.

Anna took the bread and began to eat it. It wasn't exactly a sweet pastry filled with poppy seeds and honey, but as hungry as she was, it tasted almost as good. When she finished the bread, she lay back on the hay and was soon asleep.

"Helena! Anna! Soldiers are coming up the road. They're almost here. Hurry!"

Anna was not yet fully awake, when she felt herself being half carried, half pulled along, by her father.

"Quickly. Quickly," her father whispered urgently. "This way. There is a door at the back. This way."

As they stumbled in the dark toward the small door, Anna could hear the sound of a heavy truck coming up the dirt road. It came to a stop in front of the barn, just as Anna, her parents, and Uncle Juliusz hurried out the back door and began to run across the open field. A short distance away was the dark safety of the trees.

"This way," whispered Uncle Juliusz, as he ran. "Stay together." Seconds later, they entered the woods. Holding tight to her father's hand, Anna ran and stumbled. Branches tore at their clothes and their skin, but they ran on. Once, Anna fell, but her father dragged her on, even as she tried desperately to get to her feet. She could hear the distant shouting of the soldiers as they searched the barn.

"Hurry!" cried her father. "Hurry!"

Anna ran through the woods as fast as she could, until she felt she could run no farther. Her legs ached and a sharp pain stabbed her side. Then, just as Anna felt she had run as far as she could, she heard Uncle Juliusz cry out, "There it is! Rumania. The border!"

A moment later and they were at the edge of the woods. They were exhausted, cold, and frightened, but they were — for the moment — safe.

It was then, as they stood at the edge of the woods, trying to catch their breath and decide what to do next, that Anna realized she wasn't carrying her blue sweater. Her heart pounded wildly. Tears stung her eyes. "The crèche!" Anna sobbed. "I left it in the barn! Grandpa's crèche. It's gone.... It's gone forever."

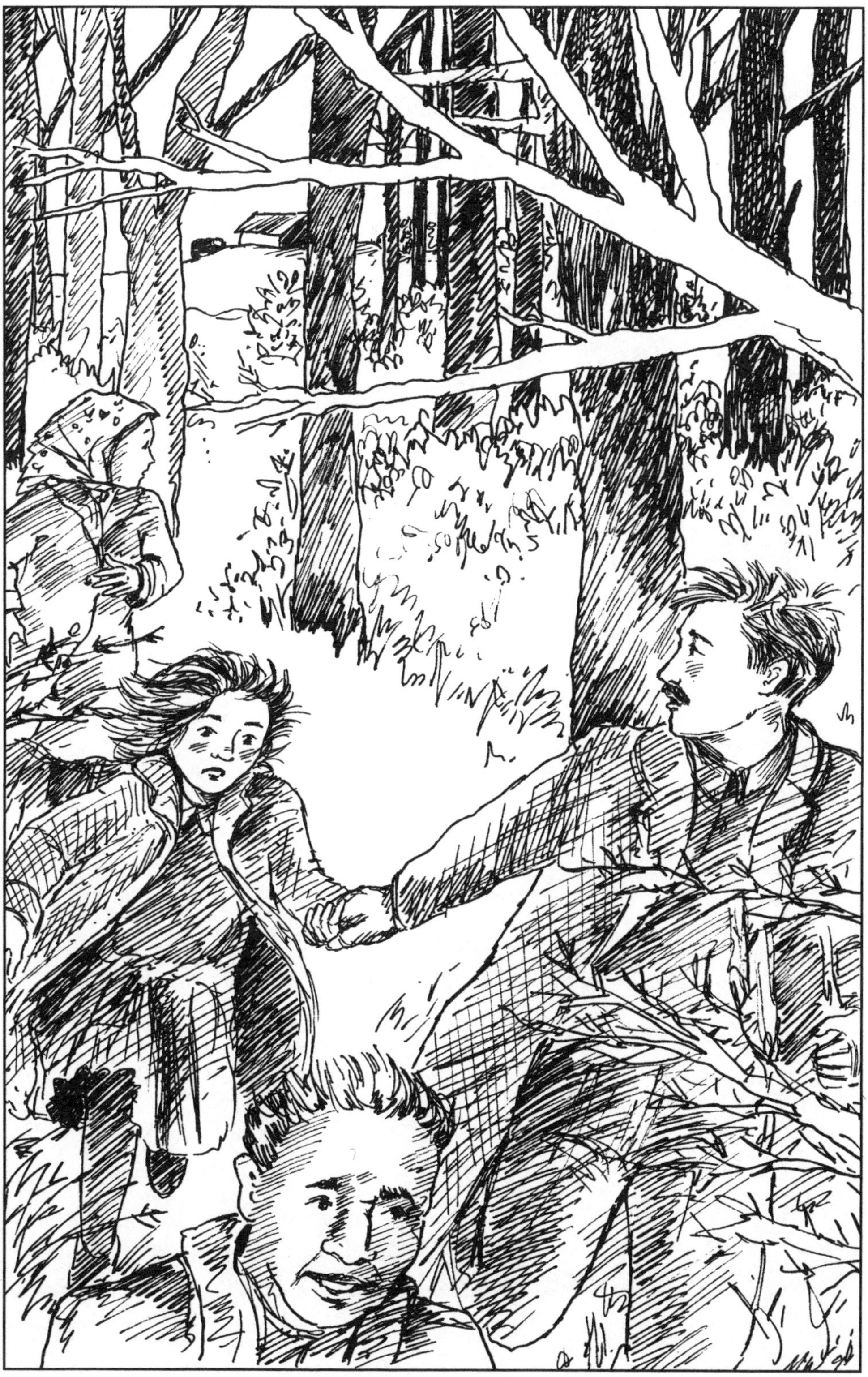

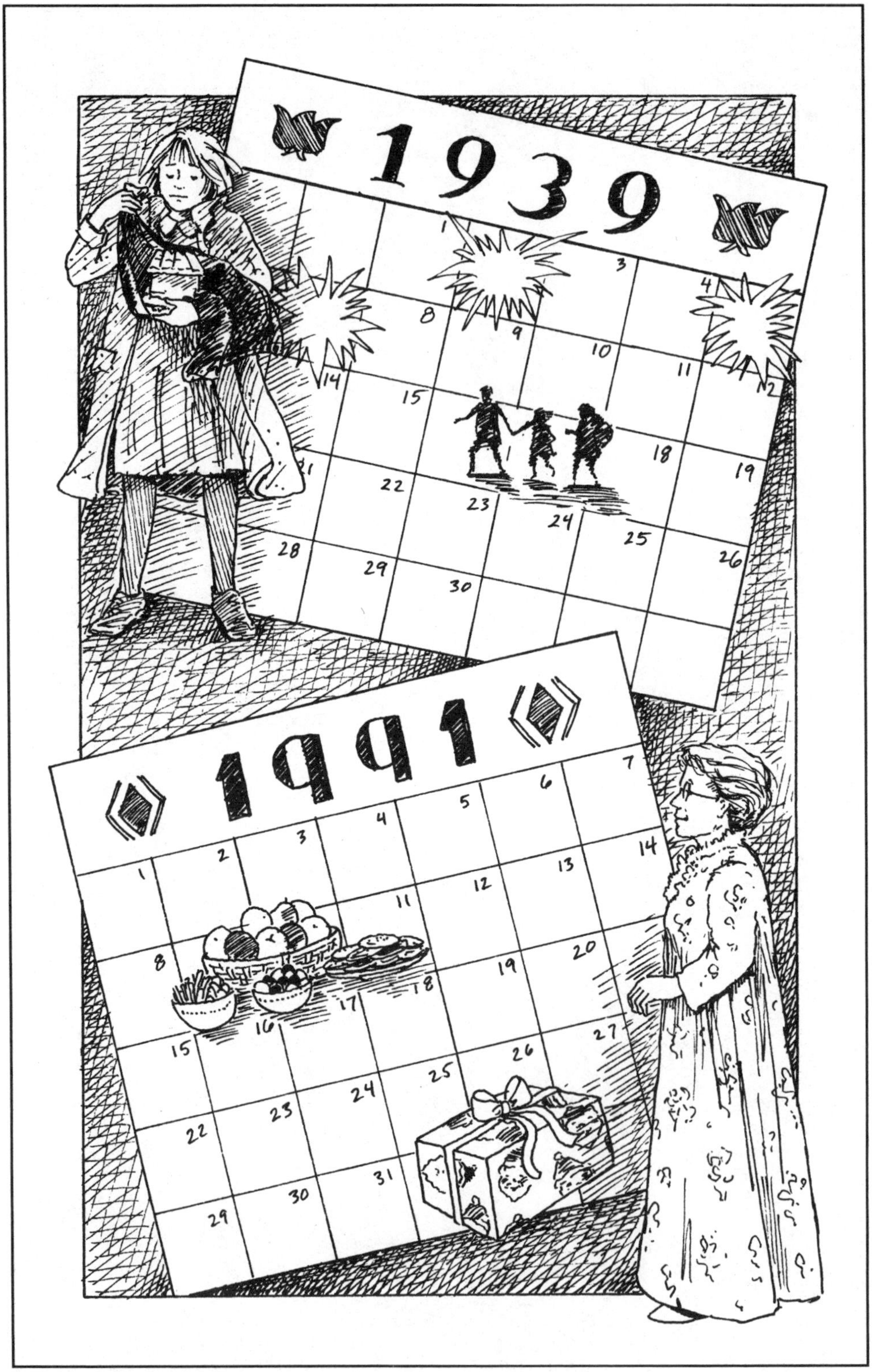
1939
1991

Part III

"The Gift"

Michigan, 1991

"Good grief!" said Lisa, rolling her eyes in disbelief. "You aren't *actually* going to give that old thing to Grandma Anna, are you?"

Katie frowned, but didn't answer her cousin. She knew there was no point in arguing, especially when Lisa was in one of her snobby, show-offy moods. Instead, she concentrated on carefully folding several large sheets of white tissue paper around the small wooden crèche. It was difficult to do — the sheets of tissue paper were large and awkward to handle, while the crèche was small and oddly shaped. But, after several minutes of concentrated effort, she managed to fold and tape the paper around it.

When she was done, she carefully placed the package in a large pink shoe box, in which her Aunt Celia ordinarily kept her boots. The box was a bit large, but it was all that Katie could find, and it would have to do. She put the cover on and fastened it shut with two long strips of tape.

"Would you like to know what *I* got Grandma?" asked Lisa, giving the pink box a disapproving look.

'Not particularly,' thought Katie, 'but you'll probably tell me anyway.'

"Well, I'll tell you anyway," said Lisa. "I got her the most *gorgeous* lavender silk scarf you've ever seen. Grandma is going to absolutely love it. I'd show it to you, but Mom had it wrapped at the store."

'Oh, great!' thought Katie. 'Even her wrapping is going to look terrific.'

"And we got a really neat box," continued Lisa, giving the pink shoe box another one of her special looks. But Katie was only half listening as she carefully folded Christmas wrapping paper around the sides of the box. Santa faces with twinkling eyes smiled up at her.

"Put your finger on the knot while I tie a bow," said Katie.

"Good grief! Are you *actually* going to use that paper? It's gross! And yarn? You're *actually* going to use *yellow yarn* to tie your package? Why don't you use ribbon and a real bow?"

"Because I don't *have* any ribbon, and I don't *have* a bow, and I *like* it the way it is," said Katie, pulling the yarn tight and catching the tip of Lisa's finger in the knot.

"Ouch! That hurt!" complained Lisa, shaking the pinched finger.

"Sorry," said Katie, as she finished the bow. "There," she said, "it's done. What do you think of it?"

Lisa looked at the package and shrugged. "Well," she sighed, "it's the thought that counts." And with that, she spun around and skipped toward the door. "I'll see you tonight at Grandma's," she called over her shoulder. "Mom got me the neatest dress you ever saw, and I've got to go home and change."

Left alone, Katie began to feel uneasy. Although she knew Lisa could be an awful snob, she began to wonder if her cousin was right. Maybe her present really wasn't any good. Was the crèche just an "old thing," as Lisa had said? Katie stared at the oversized box, with its smiling Santa faces and yellow yarn, and thought about the crèche hidden inside. Why, she wondered now, had she bought it? She remembered how excited she was when she first spotted it at her school's Christmas bazaar. It had cost nearly

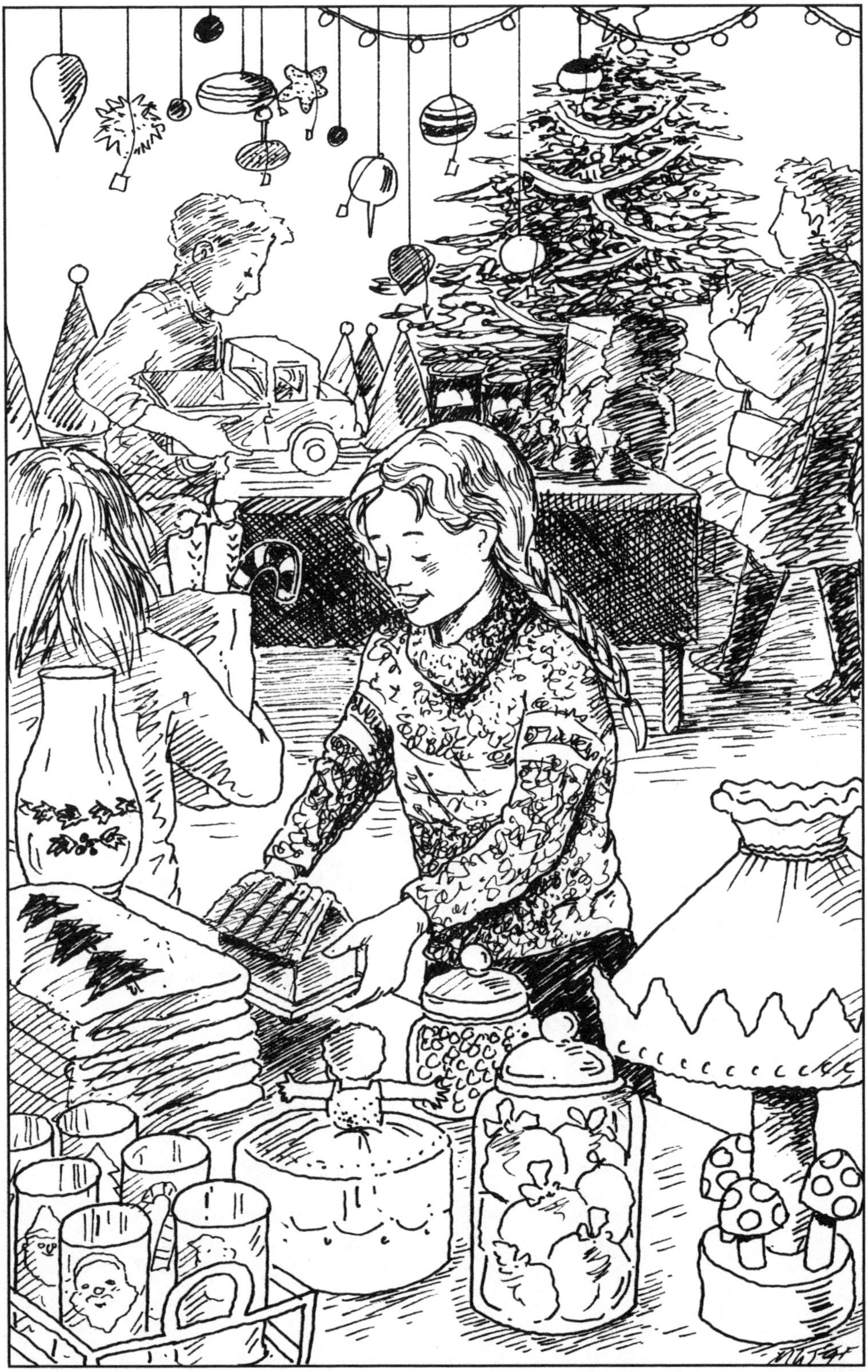

half the money she had left, but as soon as she saw it, she knew she wanted to buy it for Grandma Anna. It was just too special to leave. And she just knew Grandma Anna would love it. Now, though, after half an hour of Lisa's taunting, she wasn't so sure, and now it was too late. Suddenly, Katie felt awfully depressed. She loved Grandma Anna so very much, and wanted more than anything to give her just the right gift. But what had she done? She had gone and bought an old wooden crèche.

"Lisa's right," she said, talking to herself. "It *is* all dusty, and it *does* look like it's a hundred years old!"

Katie's thoughts were suddenly interrupted by the chiming of the hall clock. She counted the low gong-like sounds. There were five, and Katie knew she had better get ready. She reached into her closet for the new red dress she had just received for her tenth birthday. Katie had been looking forward to wearing it for Christmas Eve. Grandma Anna loved it, and said it reminded her of a beautiful red dress she had when she was just about Katie's age. "But," she said, "I never got a chance to wear it." And there was a sad, far-away look in her eyes.

As Katie pulled the dress over her head, her mother called from downstairs, "Hurry up, everyone. Remember, Grandma is expecting us before the first star appears."

Katie recalled how last year she and her brother and all their cousins sat silently in front of Grandma Anna's large living room windows and waited for the first star of the evening to appear. As Grandma Anna had explained, the first star was the sign that the Christmas festivities could begin.

"When I was a young girl in Poland," Grandma Anna told them, "all the children would begin to search the sky as soon as the sun had set. Each one wanted to be the first in their house to see the very first star on Christmas Eve. Once," she said, "I was the first one to see it, and I remember how terribly excited I was and how I shouted, 'I see it! I see it!' And everyone looked. And my father said, 'Yes. Anna is right! It is the first star.' And then everyone shouted, 'Merry Christmas! Merry Christmas!' Then we went into the dining room, where my mother had prepared the most wonderful Christmas dinner."

'Tonight,' thought Katie, as she looked at herself in the full-length mirror that hung on the back of her bedroom door, '*I'm* going to see the first star, just like Grandma did.'

"Mom, have you seen my other blue sock?" called Katie's brother. "I can only find one."

"Look on your aquarium stand," Katie's mother called back. "I believe I saw a navy-blue sock hanging from it a little while ago."

Katie giggled when she heard her mother's answer. Her brother's room was always a mess — a real disaster area. She giggled some more when she thought about the present she had gotten for him at the Christmas bazaar. It was a sign for his bedroom door that said, "DANGER - ENTER AT OWN RISK!"

★ ★ ★ ★

As her father turned into the driveway, Katie thought her grandparents' house looked just like a Christmas card. The roof, lawn, and trees were all white with snow. On the front door was a large wreath of dark-green pine boughs. And through one of the living room windows, Katie could see the twinkling lights of a Christmas tree.

She remembered how last year Uncle Joe had urged Grandma and Grandpa to sell the house. "It's much too big for only two people," he said. "In an apartment, there's no maintenance, and no lawns to mow. It's wonderful." But Grandma and Grandpa decided to ignore Uncle Joe's advice and went right on enjoying their beautiful old house. And Katie was glad. She had hoped that her grandparents would not sell the house and move into a small apartment. 'It just wouldn't be the same,' Katie thought. 'Christmas, especially, just wouldn't be the same.'

"Come in, come in," cried Grandma Anna and Grandpa together, as Katie, her parents, and brother entered the house. And then, as each new group of relatives arrived, the living room was filled with shouts of, "Come in, come in. Merry Christmas, Merry Christmas," followed by hugs and kisses and handshakes and pats on the back and laughter and crying babies and giggling and sudden shouts and running children and all sorts of wonderful noise and music and colors and lights. And wonderful smells — the smell of pine branches and spices and perfume and scented candles and baking pies and peppermint candies. And then, as soon as it became a little quieter, the doorbell would ring, and a moment later, the whole wonderful noisy scene would be repeated all over again. This continued until the very last relative arrived and the whole family was assembled at Grandma Anna's house.

To Katie, it was all absolutely perfect — the most wonderful, the most magical, the most glorious night of the year. Christmas Eve.

★ ★ ★ ★

As each new group of children arrived at

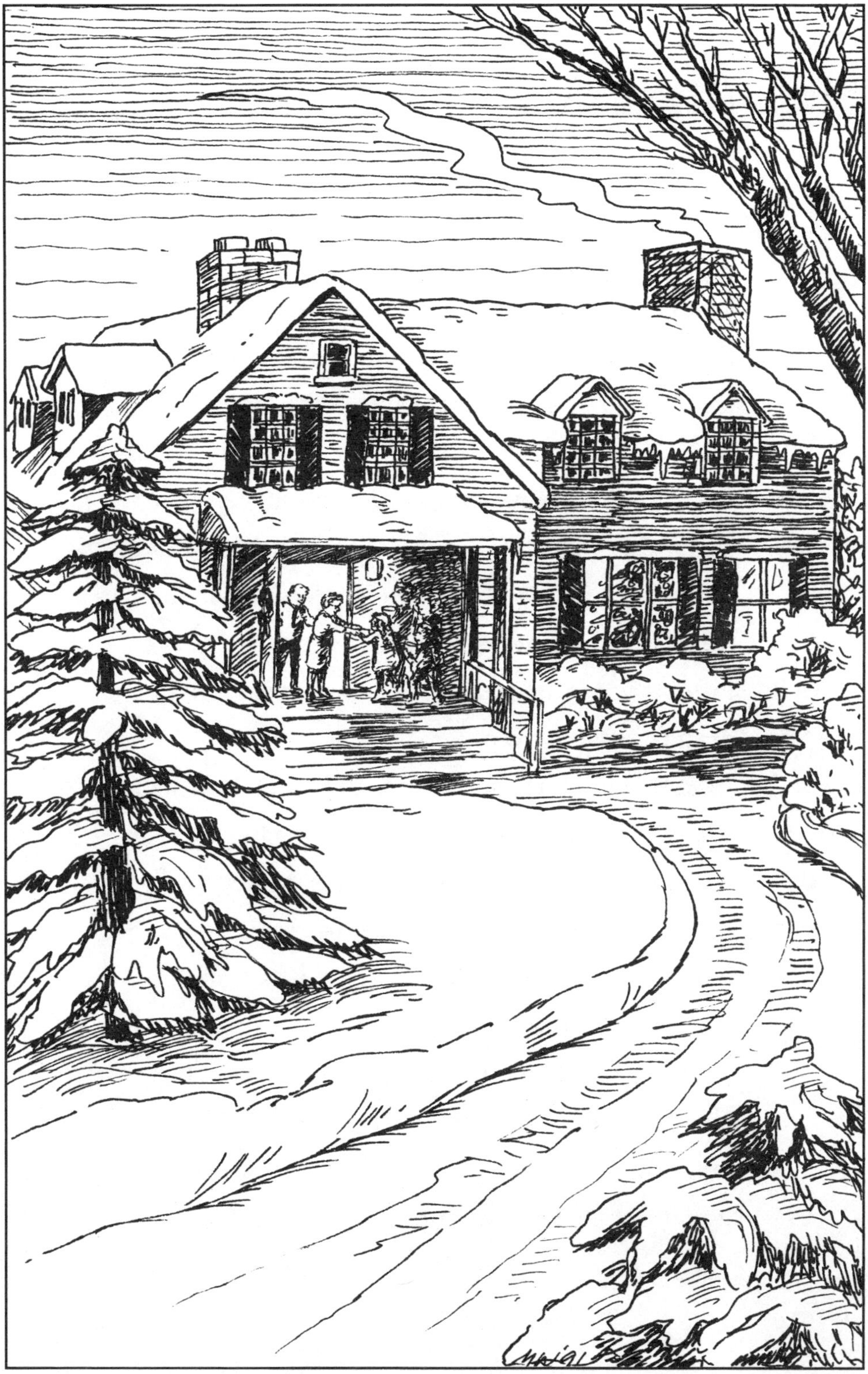

the house, they ran at once to the living room, where they crowded together before the large picture windows that faced the front lawn. Soon, a dozen noses pressed against the icy glass, as the children searched the darkening sky for the first star of the evening. Katie stared intently at the sky, determined that this year she would be the first to see the star. After a while, Grandma Anna came over and stood beside her, and she too looked up into the night sky, just as she had done so many years ago in Poland. For a moment, Katie thought she saw tears in her grandmother's eyes.

"The star! I see it! I see it! It's the first star! There it is. There, to the right of the big tree, at the top. See it?" It was Lisa who was shouting so excitedly, and everyone looked to the right of the big tree, at the top, and all agreed that she had indeed seen the first star of the evening. Katie was excited, but disappointed as well. 'It figures,' she thought. 'First it's a lavender silk scarf and now *this*. And I just know Grandma Anna is going to hate my present.'

Part IV

"Christmas Eve"

Michigan, 1991

"Merry Christmas, everyone," cried Grandma Anna. "Merry Christmas to you all. And now that Lisa has seen the first star of the evening, let us all celebrate together." And with that wonderful invitation, the whole family — grandparents, sons, daughters, nieces, nephews, aunts, uncles, cousins...everyone — moved toward the dining room, where two long tables, covered with white tablecloths, stood waiting. And everywhere — beneath the tablecloths, on the mantel and china cabinet, in the corners of the room, and over the doorways — were decorative shocks and sprays of wheat, hay, and straw, to remind everyone that the little baby whose birthday they were celebrating that night was born in a stable.

Then, after everyone was seated, and Grandpa had said a prayer, the Christmas feast began. And what a feast it was. There were huge bowls of hot and cold soup, and large platters of steaming fish, covered with thick creamy sauces. And there were vegetables — ruby-red beets and boiled potatoes and cabbage and sliced carrots and dark-green spinach and yellow and orange squash and green and yellow beans and turnips and fat brown mushrooms. And there were salads of lettuce and cucumbers and radishes and celery and tomatoes — all sparkling with vinegar and lemon juice. And there were little bowls of sour cream and honey and chopped horseradish and salted butter. And there were trays of fruits and nuts — apples and pears and oranges and raisins and heaps of almonds and walnuts. And there were all kinds of breads — white bread and dark brown wheat bread and rye bread spiced with caraway seeds and fancy rolls all twisted in knots and covered with tiny bits of onion and poppy seeds. And there were dishes filled with cinnamon and peppermint candies. And there were cakes and pies and cookies and pastries, including Katie's favorite — a pastry filled to overflowing with poppy seeds and honey.

And there was more — the hearty laughter and storytelling of Katie's aunts and uncles, the excited giggles of her cousins, the wonderful aromas and smells of Grandma Anna's cooking, and all the many different and delicious tastes. And then, when the wonderful dinner was over, Katie felt so full — so stuffed — that she thought she would surely burst if she took even one more bite.

"And now that we've had our dinner," said Grandma Anna, "it is time to open our gifts."

This announcement was greeted with the applause and excited laughter of the children, and soon the entire family was once again assembled in the living room. Then, one by one, the packages, which had been placed under the Christmas tree, were handed out and opened. As each gift was displayed, it was greeted with smiles of appreciation and pleasure, and there were hugs and kisses and laughter.

Then Grandma Anna had Lisa's gift on her lap. She carefully removed the silver bow and ribbon and the shiny, gold-foil wrapping paper. She removed the cover, parted the folds of white tissue paper, and lifted out a beautiful lavender silk scarf.

"Oh, how absolutely lovely," said Grandma Anna. "Thank you, Lisa, dear. I love it."

Lisa sent an 'I knew she'd love it' look over to Katie.

Katie squirmed uncomfortably. She

looked over at the few remaining presents. And there, behind a low hanging branch of the Christmas tree, was the large box with the smiling Santas and the bright yellow yarn. 'Maybe, somehow, I can get it back and hide it,' thought Katie. 'Then, later, after Christmas, I can get Grandma something *really* nice...something she'd really like. Maybe, I....' But it was too late.

"Here, Grandma," said Lisa, smiling sweetly, "open this one. It's from Katie."

Grandma Anna took the package and placed it on her lap. Then, as everyone watched, she slowly and carefully untied the yellow yarn. She removed the smiling Santa wrapping paper, lifted off the bright pink cover, and carefully unfastened the taped folds of white tissue paper. Then, as Katie held her breath, Grandma Anna folded back the layers of soft, white paper.

For a long moment, Grandma Anna simply sat still and stared down at the large pink box on her lap. Then, slowly, she looked up. Her face was filled with surprise, confusion, and disbelief. Katie could hardly breathe. 'Is it *that* bad?' she wondered. 'Is Grandma *that* disappointed?'

"Katie," said Grandma, in a hoarse whisper, "how...where...is it possible?" And then, as her eyes filled with tears, she looked down again at the large box on her lap. Everyone in the room was silent as they looked first at Grandma Anna, then at Katie, and then back at Grandma Anna. Her hands were shaking as she slowly and carefully lifted the fragile crèche from the tissue paper wrapping. Tears rolled down her cheeks as she gently touched each tiny figure — the Holy Baby, Mary, Joseph, four lambs, a cow, and a donkey.

"It's a miracle," she said, softly. "It's a miracle." And with the tip of her finger she carefully traced the ornately carved M, with its swirls and curves. Grandma Anna looked up at the family, and in a voice filled with both laughter and tears, she said, "It is Grandpa Malek's crèche." Then, with her eyes closed, and with tears streaming down her cheeks, she cried, "Oh, Grandpa Malek... my beautiful crèche has been

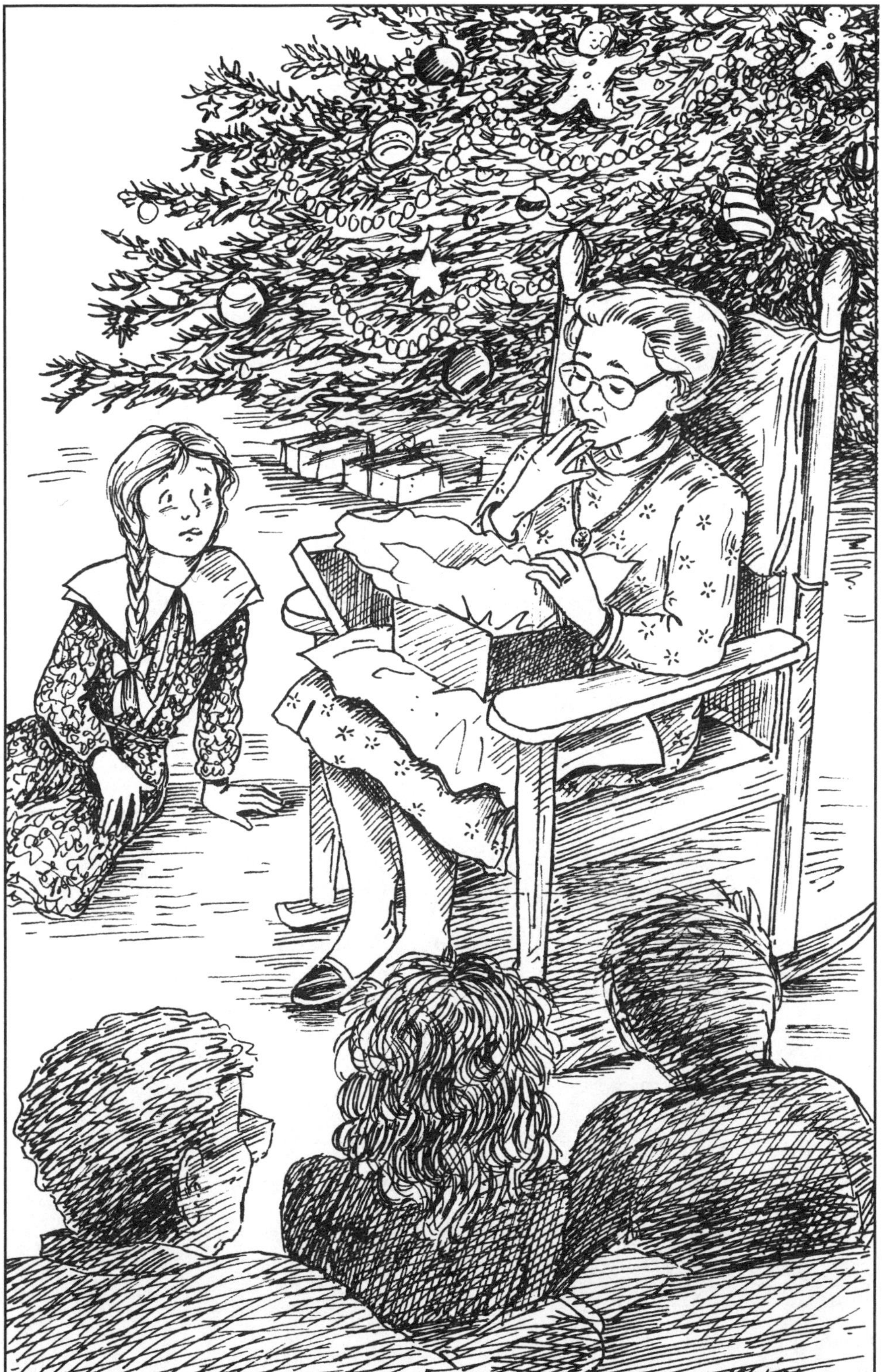

found.... And, this time, I *promise* you, I won't *ever* lose it again."

"Anna, Anna," whispered her husband. "What is it, dear? What's wrong? Don't cry, please...everything will be all right." But by now Grandma Anna was completely overcome with emotion, and as Grandpa held her, she cried uncontrollably.

Everyone sat in stunned silence. Katie and Lisa looked at each other, their eyes brimming with tears — all thoughts of competition completely gone.

★ ★ ★ ★

Later, after her tears were gone, Grandma Anna placed the little wooden crèche on the mantel above the fireplace. And then, as everyone crowded together around her chair, she told them of her home in Poland, and of how her grandfather, Joseph Malek, had given her this very same crèche one special Christmas Eve, more than fifty years ago. She told the family — Joseph Malek's family — all about him. She told them what a good and kind man he was, and how very much she loved him. She told them about the war, and how she and her parents had to flee Krakow in the middle of the night, how she had taken the crèche with her, how they hid in a barn, and how they had to run through the woods to escape from the soldiers, and how, when they reached the Rumanian border, she discovered that she had left the crèche behind, and thought that it was lost forever.

"All these years, I have wondered what happened to it. And all these years, I have wanted so much to see it once more."

Then, as Grandma Anna finished her story, she and Katie looked at each other and smiled.

★ ★ ★ ★

The house was still. Only the memories of all the joy and laughter and tears remained. Grandpa slept deeply and peacefully in his large oak bed, and the only sounds to be heard were his heavy breathing and the faint ticking of the tall clock that stood in the darkened hallway. In the living room, on the mantel above the fireplace, stood the small wooden crèche, and before it, stood Grandma Anna. As she looked at the tiny wooden figures, she remembered the terrible night when she stood in the doorway and said a tearful, final good-bye to her little room. And she remembered the long days and nights of traveling through the Polish countryside, and the terrifying race through the woods, and, finally, the painful realization that she had left the precious crèche behind. And now, after so many years, there it was — so small, so fragile, so old, and yet, so beautiful. 'But how did it survive?' She wondered. 'Who found it, and how did it come to America? To little Katie? And to me?'

"It is a miracle," she whispered to herself. "It is a miracle."

But even as Anna looked at the little crèche, at the tiny figures of Mary and Joseph and the Baby, the four lambs and the cow and the

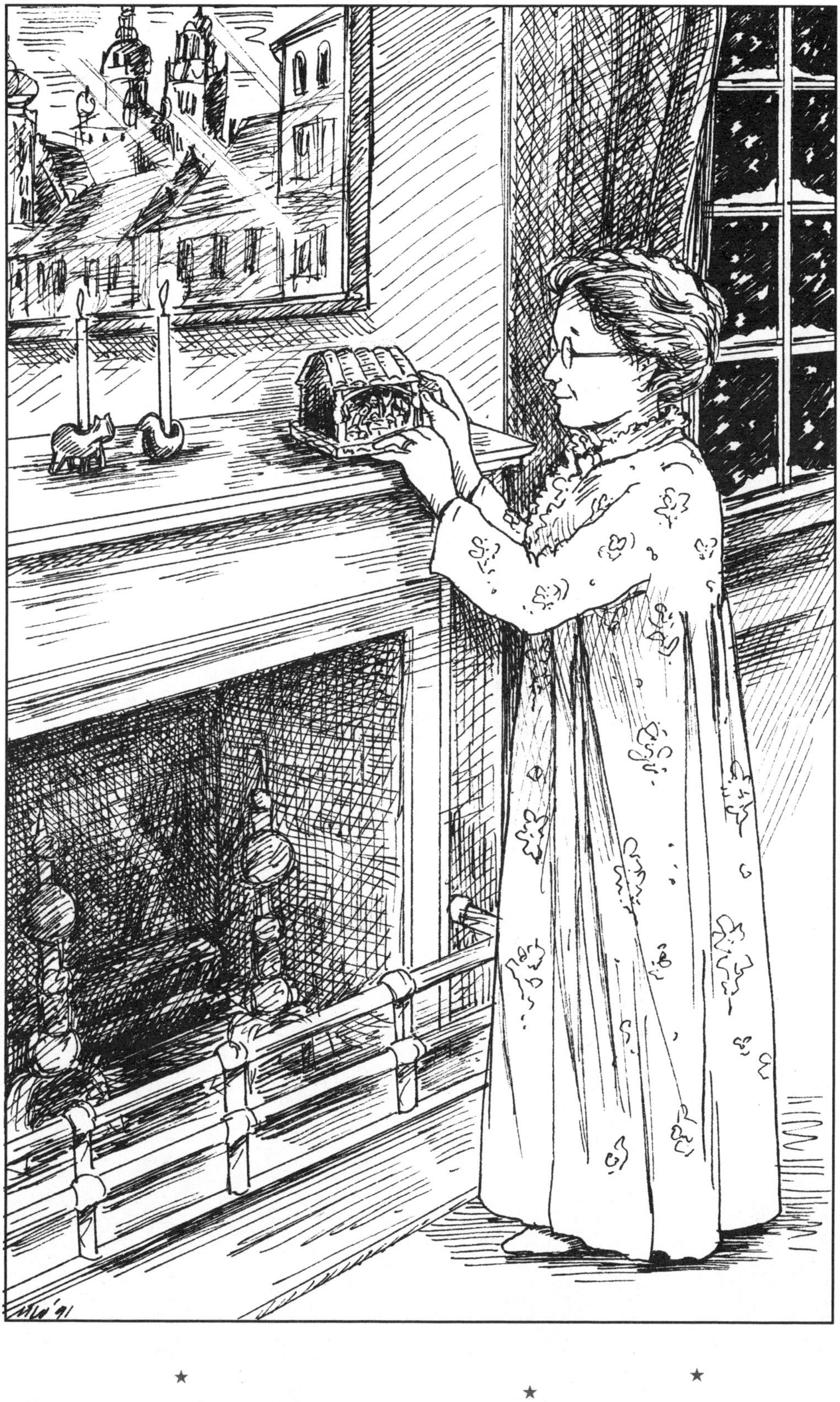

donkey, she saw in the tiny scene the *real* miracle of Christmas — the miracle of hope — hope for the future, hope for a world at peace, hope for a world filled only with love and joy. And hope, as Anna now knew, can never die, for it is reborn in our hearts each Christmas with the birth of the Holy Child, and it will endure forever.

Grandma Anna's Favorite Christmas Cookies
Honey Cookies
(Pierniki)

(Note: Honey has long been a favorite ingredient in Polish cooking. As a result, much of the Polish countryside is dotted with beehives.)

Ingredients

½ cup honey	½ tsp. ginger
½ cup sugar	½ tsp. vanilla (extract)
2 eggs	½ tsp. salt
3 cups flour	¼ tsp. cloves
1 tsp. baking soda	1 egg white (beaten)
½ tsp. cinnamon	Approx. 4 dozen almond halves,
½ tsp. nutmeg	parboiled or blanched

Directions
1. Combine honey and sugar in a small bowl and mix well. Beat in eggs and vanilla. Set aside.
2. In a separate bowl, blend flour, baking soda, and salt. Add cinnamon, ginger, nutmeg, and cloves, and blend well.
3. Add blended flour and spices to honey mixture. Stir well until dough is formed, then knead thoroughly to ensure uniform mixture of ingredients.
4. When dough stiffens, cover and set aside for approx. 2-2 ½ hours.
5. Roll out dough on flour-covered surface. When dough is approx. ¼″ thick, cut into 2 ½″ shapes — rounds, stars, etc.
6. Using a pastry brush, lightly coat cookies with egg white. Press one almond half into the surface of each cookie. Place cookies on greased cookie sheet and bake at 375° F for 8-10 minutes. When done, cool on cookie racks. Store cookies in a tightly covered cookie jar. Enjoy! (Note: Recipe should yield approx. 48 cookies.)

Cream Cheese Cookies
(Kolacky)

Ingredients
2 ¼ cups flour
1-8 oz. package cream cheese
1 cup butter
¼ tsp. vanilla (extract)
½ tsp. salt
Canned fruit filling (such as prune, apricot, etc.) or thick jam of choice
Powdered or confectioners' sugar

Directions
1. In a medium-size bowl, combine butter and cream cheese; stir or mix until fluffy. Blend in vanilla, salt, and flour. Mix well. When dough forms, cover and place in refrigerator for 2-3 hours.
2. Roll out dough on floured surface until dough is approx. ¼" - ½" thick. Using a small glass, press out 2"-2 ½" circles or rounds. Arrange cookies on ungreased baking or cookie sheets.
3. Press a "thumbprint" about ¼" deep into the surface of each cookie. Fill each depression with jam or fruit filling of choice.
4. Bake at 350°F for 12-15 minutes or until golden brown. Remove from oven and dust cookies with a light coating of confectioners' sugar. Cool on cookie racks. Then ... yum, yum! (Note: Recipe should yield approx. 3 ½ dozen cookies.)